Hamza and Khadija

And the yummy berries

Written by

Abeda Sultana

They thanked Allah and said the dua **"Alhamdu lillaa hilladhee ahyaanaa..."**

2

They went to the kitchen
and sat on their chairs.

Their mum gave them
yummy breakfast to eat,
some waffles and milk,
a lovely treat.

6

When they had finished, Hamza stood up
to wash his hands, his plate and his cup.
As he was going towards the sink
he dropped his dishes in a blink.

Then re-assured Hamza and
gave him kisses.

She held them tight and then she mentioned,
"Your actions are according to your intentions".

She hugged them both
and explained while they stood
**"Always plan to do something good,
even if you don't end up doing it,
you will still get rewarded for planning
and thinking it".**

Then their mum told them
that they were going out later
to visit Mrs May, their elderly neighbour.

Then she thought of a great idea,
to pick some berries to give to her later.

13

They ran upstairs and got dressed quickly they were very excited, they set out happily.

14

There was a berry farm not too far.
Looked after by a man
who was the farmer.
They approached the farm
and walked inside.
They saw a selection of berries,
some raw and some dried.

15

The farmer asked what sort of berries they'd like,
he showed them ones that were ready and ripe.

There were strawberries, raspberries and cranberries too,
but their favourite were the berries which look blue.

Hamza and Khadija picked a basket full of **blueberries!!**

They looked so juicy
and looked so yummy.

They thanked the farmer
for helping them choose
the perfect berries so they didn't get confused.

20

Hamza and Khadija were so happy and excited that they would give Mrs May the berries so she would be delighted.

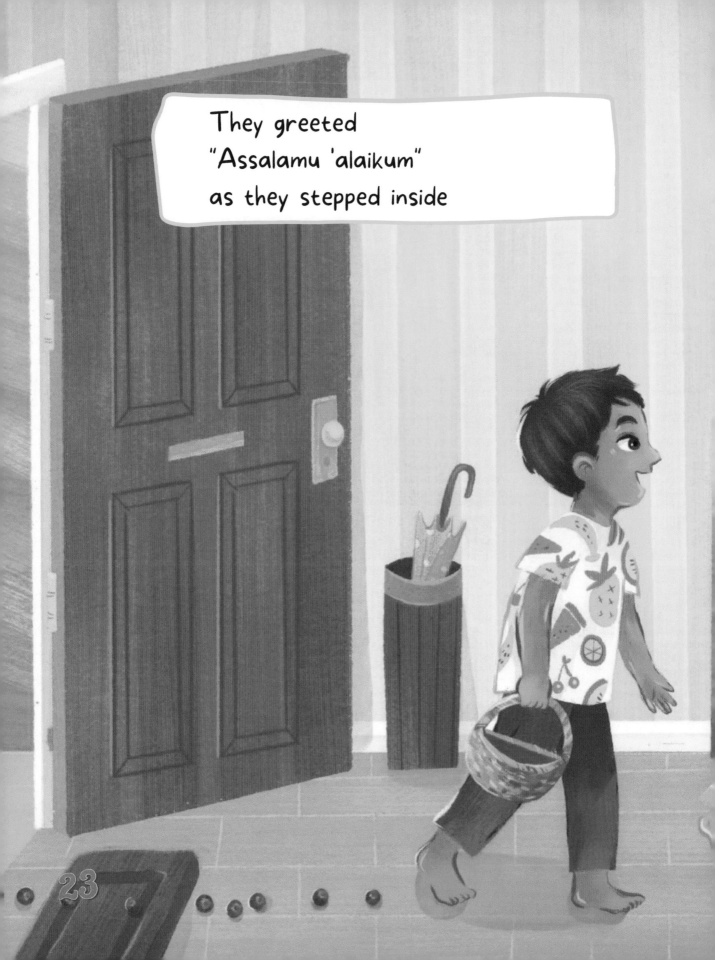

"Wa 'alaikum salam" their mum replied.

Their mum said to them "We have a visitor today, our neighbour Mrs May, she went to the hospital and stopped by on the way".

Hamza and Khadija were glad to see
Their elderly neighbour sitting there
so comfortably.

26

They reached out to give the basket to their neighbour which seemed less bulky and alot lighter.
They looked inside and was shocked to see that the basket had ripped and was completely empty!

27

Khadija explained to Mrs May feeling unhappy
"We picked some berries for you
because you were poorly".

Mrs May was delighted for the lovely gesture.
She said "Thank you for the thought"
and gave them closure.
She hugged them both and then she mentioned
"Your actions are according to your intentions".

28

Hamza and Khadija walked Mrs May home.
Khadija held her soft hand which felt very warm.

They went back home feeling at ease knowing that they did their best to please Allah, The Mighty Al-Aziz.

30

The End

Prophet Muhammad (Peace be upon him) said:
"Actions are according to intentions, and everyone
will get rewarded what they intend"
Bukhari & Muslim

Printed in Great Britain
by Amazon

26557096R00021